Meet
M and M

by Pat Ross
pictures by Marylin Hafner

FONTANA YOUNG LIONS

ONE

Mandy and Mimi were friends.
They were such good friends
that sometimes they pretended
to be twins.
But Mandy was two inches taller.
So she bent her legs
to look shorter.
And Mimi was one size bigger.
So she held in her stomach
to look smaller.
Then she stood on her toes
to look taller.
But . . .

They both had straight brown hair—
with tangles on the same side
where they chewed it.
They both had the same
front tooth missing.
And both their names began with M.
That was enough for them!
Every day after school,
Mandy climbed the back stairs
of the apartment building

where they both lived.

She always took two steps at a time

from her apartment 2B

to Mimi's apartment 3B.

Or Mimi hopped down the stairs

backwards for twenty hops

without stopping.

"We are the twins, M and M,"
they told everyone they met.
"We stick together like glue!"
They grew out their fringes
and looked shaggy together.
They shared fancy hair clips—
Mandy's red ones with the stars,
and Mimi's silver ones
that sparkled in the dark.

"Rub-a-dub-dub,

M and M in the tub,"

they sang at bath time.

They took turns piling bubbles

in the yellow pail

that belonged to *both* of them.

Mandy let Mimi use
her mother's new electric toothbrush.
So Mimi let Mandy try on
her mother's new velvet coat
with the tags still on.
Mandy shared Baby,
her guinea pig.
Mimi shared Maxi,
her dog.

They invented the
Haunted House Game and made
scary spiders to tape on the walls.
They played shops with
tins of food from the kitchen.
The shopper always complained
about the prices.

The girl always said,
"We do our best, lady."

They had great times
playing tricks.
They hid Maxi's doggie treats
in the umbrella stand.
Once they hid Baby
in someone's shoe.
And no one ever knew which one
had played the trick.
Sometimes people forgot
who was Mandy and who was Mimi.
Those two were always together.
"Just call us M and M,"
they would say.

TWO

One crabby day everything went wrong.
Mandy and Mimi argued
about what games to play
and how to play them.
Finally, they decided
playing cards would be fun.

But then, they argued
over *where* to play!
After that,
Mandy would not let Mimi
pet Baby on her special pillow—
not even once.
That same day, Mimi showed Mandy
her new box of markers
in twenty exciting colours.
But she only let Mandy *look*.

Before they knew it,

they had one awful fight.

"You Dummy!" screamed Mimi.

"You Big Jerk!" screamed Mandy.

Maxi barked at both of them.

And that was that.

Mimi went home to 3B.
She said she was never
ever coming back.
Mandy called out,
"Who cares?"
And she slammed the door so hard
she hit her elbow on the wall.

They knew each other's
phone number by heart.
And most of the time
when they got mad
they called back in a few minutes
and said, "Want to play?"
That always meant, "I'm sorry."
But this time the phone did not ring.

That very day Mandy hid in the curtains
and watched Mimi walk Maxi.
Later on, Mimi watched Mandy
ride her bike with Tommy from 3C.

The next day,

they met in the lift going down.

The first thing Mimi said was,

"I'm going to the circus with Tommy."

"Well, I've already been—two times,"

said Mandy.

When the lift got to the hall,

they didn't even say goodbye.

That same afternoon,

Mandy sold lemonade

on one side of the big front doors.

And Mimi sold lemonade

on the other side.

Mandy's sign said:

THE BEST IN THIS CITY!

Mimi's sign said:

MUCH BETTER!

Mandy sold one cup
for five pence.
So Mimi sold one cup
plus an extra sip
for five pence.

So Mandy sold one cup
plus an extra sip
plus a free straw
for five pence.

So Mimi sold one cup

plus an extra sip

plus a free straw

plus a song

for five pence.

Mandy thought that was silly.

And she said so.

Then she took her lemonade stand
back inside.

That night at Mimi's house
the phone rang three times.
Mimi ran to get it first.
But all three calls were
for the babysitter,
who talked to her friends all night.

That night at Mandy's house
the phone rang twice.
Mandy ran to get it first.
But not one call was for her.

THREE

On the third day, the rain came down
like a cold shower.
Mimi sat alone in her room
with Maxi in 3B.
Maxi was glad to have Mimi there.
He rubbed his sloppy mouth
all over Mimi's face
giving her kisses.

But Mimi was not in the mood
for dog kisses.
She was in the mood
for the biggest bubble bath ever.
But before long,
most of the good bubbles had gone away.
Only grey water was left,
and a dirty ring.
It was just no fun
taking a bubble bath alone.

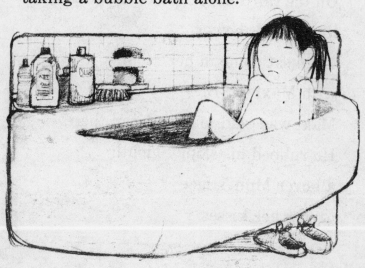

Downstairs in 2B, Mandy tried to play
the Haunted House Game alone.
But the game was not scary at all.
So she decided to play with Baby.
But Baby just slept.
Mandy got out her old, dry markers
and wet them.
But the colours were not
bright and pretty on the paper.

Tap, tap, tap.

Mandy heard a noise.

She thought it must be the rain.

But the rain had stopped.

Tap, tap, tap . . .

Mandy looked out of the window.

There, hanging from a rope,

was a yellow pail.

It was *their* yellow bathtub pail!
Mandy opened the window
and pulled the pail
over the window sill

and into her room.
There was something inside—
a flat square package
wrapped in silver foil.

Carefully, she opened the little square.

Inside was a bright picture of Maxi.

And a note that said:

TO M— DO YOU WANT A MARKER?
WHAT COLOUR?
　　　　　—FROM
　　　　　　　M.

Quickly, Mandy wet her black marker,
the only one that worked.
And she wrote back:

TO M —
How about PurPLe?
From M.

She wrapped the note in the silver foil
and put it back in the pail.

Then she put Baby's special pillow
in the pail, too.
The rope was still tight.
She gave it a little pull.
Then out the window went the pail,
and up to 3B.

A few minutes later,
down came the pail with the pillow
and a short note that said:
MAXI TRIED TO CHEW IT UP!

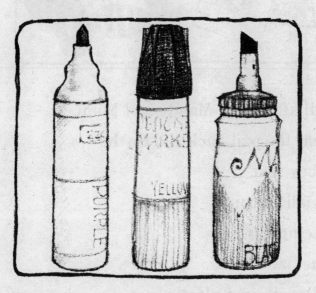

In the pail, Mandy also found
three markers—
the purple one, a yellow one,
and a black that worked.

All afternoon, Mandy and Mimi

sent the pail back and forth.

They sent

small pictures,

racing cars,

one hairbrush,

biscuits in a plastic bag,

comic books,

a puzzle with only two pieces missing,

and a million notes.

The last note from Mandy said:

Meet me on the stairs.

Mimi sent one back that said:

JUST WHAT I WAS THINKING!

Mimi raced down the back stairs,
hopping fast.
Mandy raced up the back stairs,
two at a time.

They met halfway,
where they sat and talked
about what to do
tomorrow.

THE END!

M and M
and
The Big Bag

CHAPTER ONE

Mandy and Mimi—

the two friends

who called themselves M and M—

looked carefully

at the yellow sheet of paper.

The big black letters at the top

spelled GROCERY LIST.

But it was not

just *any* grocery list.

It was a very important grocery list.

So they read it three times.

Mandy and Mimi
were going to the grocery shop
without a grown-up
for the very first time.
And the list was for them.
"This is it!" cried Mandy.
"It's about time!" cried Mimi.

The friends M and M
were ready for this day.
They could read prices and signs.
They could even read tricky words
like *cucumber* and *pizza*.

They could count their change.

And they always looked both ways

before they crossed the street.

They were ready all right—

ready to shop at The Big Bag alone.

They looked at the grocery list again.

The paper was clean and smooth.

The words were big and neat.

They read the list one more time—

GROCERY LIST

1 butter
1 bread
2 apples
1 box rubbish bags
1 milk

"That's an easy list," said Mimi.

"Nothing to it," said Mandy.

Mandy was in charge of the list.
She folded the paper
and tucked it under her belt.
Mimi was in charge of the money.
She pushed two pound notes
deep into her back pocket.
Then she wiggled and jumped
to make sure the money was safe.

"OK, let's move it!" Mimi shouted.
Mimi's dog Maxi ran to the door
and barked.
Maxi didn't want to be left behind.
"No Maxi," they said.
"You can't come."
But Maxi sat right by the door.

"OK, OK," said Mimi.

"You win.

But you'd better be good.

We're going to The Big Bag!"

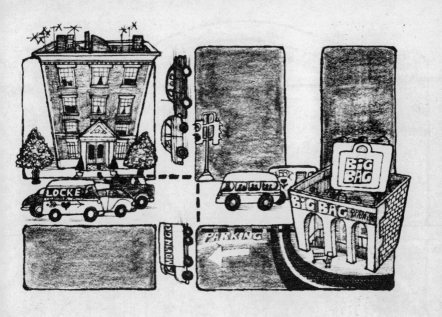

CHAPTER TWO

Mandy and Mimi
had to cross two streets
to get to The Big Bag.
One street was big and wide.
It had noisy buses and fast cars.
M and M waited
for the green man light
before they crossed the street.

The Big Bag had two front doors.

One said OUT

and NO BARE FEET.

The other said IN and

NO DOGS ALLOWED.

"That means you," said Mimi to Maxi.

Maxi didn't like being left outside—
not one bit!
He started to bark.
"Be a good dog!" said Mandy,
and she bent down to pat him.
Just then, a piece of paper—
a piece of yellow paper—
fell on the pavement

Mandy didn't see it fall.

Mimi didn't see it fall.

But Maxi did.

Maxi barked at the paper.

"Come on," said Mimi.

"Maxi always makes a fuss.

Just pretend you don't know him."

So M and M turned away

and they went into The Big Bag.

CHAPTER THREE

"What's first on the list?" asked Mimi.

Mandy reached under her belt.

"It's gone!" she cried.

"What are we going to do?"

"Who needs that list anyway?

We know what to buy," said Mimi.

"Are you sure?" asked Mandy.

She wished they had the list.

"Yes, I'm sure," said Mimi.

"I remember *everything*."

"OK," said Mandy.

She hoped that was the truth.

The Big Bag looked bigger than ever.
There were so many rows.
There were so many signs.
There was so much food.

They decided to start

with the row that said SNACKS.

"Was popcorn on the list?"

asked Mimi.

"I thought you remembered
everything," said Mandy.
"Well, I *think* it was on the list,"
said Mimi.
And she put popcorn in the trolley.
Popcorn was her favourite snack.

"What came after popcorn?"
asked Mandy.
Mimi looked at a row of sodas.
"If orange soda was not on the list,
it should have been,"
she said.
So Mandy put two orange sodas
in the trolley.

"Hey! What about that new cereal
with the free airplane inside?"
asked Mimi.
"Yeah," said Mandy.
"Grown-ups like it when you try
something new."
So Mimi put a box of Super Krunchy
in the trolley.

Soon, the trolley was filled with

popcorn,

orange soda,

cereal,

peanut butter plain,

peanut butter crunchy,

chocolate ice cream,

paper cups,

tooth brushes, and

grape bubble gum.

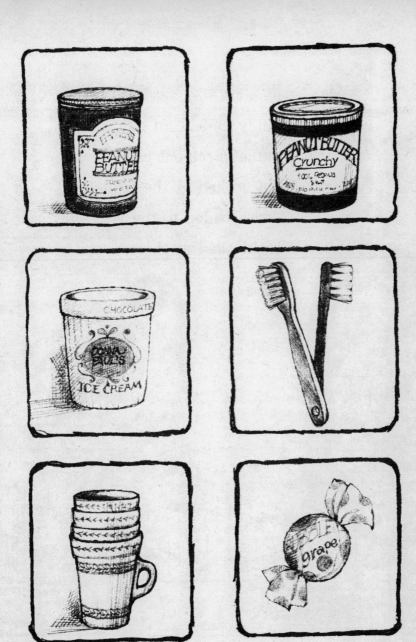

Mandy and Mimi got in line
for the check-out counter.
They looked at the trolley.
It was loaded to the very top.
They looked at the two pound
notes.

Then they looked at each other.
"We needed the list," said Mandy.
"I usually remember better,"
said Mimi.

"We'll never get to go shopping again
if we come back
with all this stuff!" cried Mandy.
"What do we do now?"
"Dump it," said Mimi.

"Dump it?" asked Mandy.

"Like this," said Mimi.

Quickly, Mimi pushed the trolley

to the back of the store—

and left it there.

They ran for the door
that said OUT.
And there was Maxi
with a yellow something
in his mouth.
"The list!" cried Mandy.
"Here Maxi," said Mimi.
Maxi chewed the paper.
"Nice Maxi," said Mimi.
Maxi still chewed the paper.
Mimi took a dog treat
out of her pocket.

Maxi dropped the paper.

Now the yellow list was

wet and slimy, sticky and dirty.

It had holes in it—

little dog-tooth holes.

"You dropped it," said Mimi.

"You pick it up."

"Yuck," said Mandy.

CHAPTER FOUR

M and M went back into

The Big Bag with the list.

The list was smelly.

And it ripped

when Mandy tried to smooth it out.

Mandy and Mimi looked

at the first word and laughed.

It said

I butt

"Butter!" said Mandy.

And they ran to get one butter.

The next word on the list
started with a dog-tooth hole.
Then came the letters r e a d.
But that did not fool them!
They knew the word was BREAD.

apples was the only whole word.
They picked out two good ones.
The next word on the list
was *rubbish*.
"This is a shop, not a dump!"
said Mandy.
Then they raced the trolley
to rubbish bags.

The last word was all rubbed out.

But Mandy and Mimi knew

the word was not popcorn

or orange soda.

They knew the word was milk.

And they picked out the coldest one.

"Well that's it," said M and M.

The man at the check-out counter
rang up each thing.
"That comes to one pound
and seventy pence," he said.

Mimi gave the clerk the two pound notes.

He gave her back thirty pence.

"Come again," said the man.

"Oh, we will!" they answered.

They ran outside and untied Maxi.

Then they gave him the list.

"It's all yours now," said Mandy.

And Maxi chewed the list right up!

Then M and M took turns carrying
one butter, one bread, two apples,
rubbish bags, and one milk
home without stopping!

MEET M AND M first published 1980
in USA by Pantheon Books
M AND M AND THE BIG BAG first published 1981
in USA by Pantheon Books

First published as one volume
in Great Britain in Fontana Lions 1983
by William Collins Sons and Co Ltd
8 Grafton Street
London W1

Printed in Great Britain
at the University Press, Oxford